THE LITTLEST DRAGON
AT SCHOOL

Also by Margaret Ryan

The Littlest Dragon
The Littlest Dragon Gets the Giggles
The Littlest Dragon Goes for Goal

THE LITTLEST DRAGON AT SCHOOL

by Margaret Ryan

Illustrated by Jamie Smith

Collins

An imprint of HarperCollinsPublishers

For Susie, with love

First published by Collins 2000
Collins is an imprint of HarperCollins*Publishers* Ltd
77-85 Fulham Palace Road, Hammersmith,
London, W6 8JB

The HarperCollins website address is:
www.**fire**and**water**.com

3 5 7 9 8 6 4

Text copyright © Margaret Ryan 2000
Illustrations copyright © Jamie Smith 2000

ISBN 0 00 675542 9

The author and illustrator assert the moral right to be
identified as the author and illustrator of the work.

Printed and bound in Great Britain by
Omnia Books Ltd, Glasgow

Conditions of Sale
This book is sold subject to the condition that it shall not, by way of trade
or otherwise, be lent, re-sold, hired out or otherwise circulated without
the publisher's prior written consent in any form of binding or cover other
than that in which it is published and without a similar condition
including this condition being imposed on the subsequent purchaser.

CONTENTS

THE LITTLEST DRAGON
AT SCHOOL

It was hardly dawn, but the littlest
dragon was wide awake.

"Time to get up. School starts
today," he yelled to his nine
big brothers, who were still asleep in
the big dragons' bed.

But the nine big dragons carried
on snoring.

"Time to get up," yelled the littlest
dragon again, and he hopped,
skipped and jumped all over them.

"Get off. It's far too early,
Number Ten," said biggest dragon
brother, Number One.

"Go away. It's still the middle of
the night, Number Ten,"
mumbled big dragon brother,
Number Two.

"If you jump on me again, I'll
hang you up by your tail,
Number Ten," growled big dragon
brother, Number Three, who was a
grumpy box in the morning.

"Go back to sleep, Number Ten," muttered all the other dragon brothers.

But the littlest dragon was too excited to go back to sleep.

He jumped off the bed, ran to the big chest in the dragons' cave, and put on his new school uniform. Then he looked at himself in the big mirror.

"What a smart looking dragon," he said. "Now to pack my school bag."

He went to the cupboard in the big
cave kitchen and found two green
apples, two packets of crisps and
two red lollipops. He was just about
to pack them into his school bag
when...

"I thought I could smell green apples," said big dragon brother, Number One.

"I love sneezy pepper crisps," said big dragon brother, Number Two.

"Red lollipops are my favourite," said big dragon brother, Number Three.

And they ate the lot.

The littlest dragon was left with two apple cores, two empty crisp packets and two lollipop sticks.

"What about my food for break time?" he said.

"You're too little to eat all that food," laughed his big brothers, and went back to bed.

"We'll see about that," muttered the littlest dragon, and had another look in the big cupboard.

He found three oranges, three
fairy cakes and three boxes of
juice. He was just about to pack
them into his school bag when...

"I thought I could smell oranges," said big dragon brother, Number Seven.

"I love fairy cakes," said big dragon brother, Number Eight.

"I could drink a whole bucket full of juice," said big dragon brother, Number Nine.

And they scoffed the lot. The littlest dragon was left with orange peel, cake crumbs and empty juice boxes.

"What about my food for break time?" he said.

"You're too little to eat all that food," laughed his big brothers, and went back to bed.

"We'll see about that," muttered
the littlest dragon, and looked in
the cupboard again.

This time all he could find were four grapes and four chocolate biscuits. He was just about to pack them into his school bag when...

"I thought I could smell grapes," said big dragon brother, Number Four.

"We love chocolate biscuits," said twins, Five and Six.

And they polished off the lot. The littlest dragon was left with nothing at all.

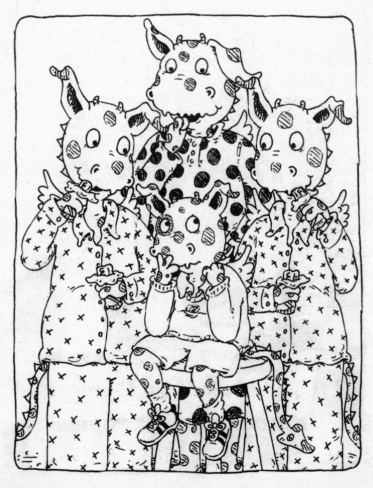

"What about my food for break time?" he said.

"You're too little to eat all that food," laughed his big brothers, and went back to bed.

The littlest dragon had another look in the big kitchen cupboard, but it was bare.

"Now what am I going to do?" he wondered.

Then he had his first idea.

"I'll look in the fridge," he said.

The fridge was full of school tuck boxes, all neatly labelled. The littlest dragon took out the one that said Number Ten.

Inside, his mum had
packed one brown-
bread sandwich,
two tangerines and
three jelly dragon sweets.

The littlest dragon grinned and
packed his tuck box into his school
bag. That gave him his second idea.

"I must pack my little football too," he said.

He went to the big cupboard in the hall where all the odds and ends were kept and found his little football. Beside it was an old burst football. That gave him his third idea.

He tiptoed to the back door of the cave where all his big dragon brothers' school bags were lined up, and searched through them. When he found the one with the big football inside, he changed it for the burst one. Then he laughed and ran off to school early.

In school he made ten sand pies,
drew ten red apples, and learned a
song about ten green dragons sitting
on a wall.

Then it was break time and he went out into the playground with his tuck box, his football, and his little dragon friends. He was just finishing off his last jelly dragon sweet when...

"Disaster!" cried his big dragon brothers rushing up to him.

"Number One's brought the old burst ball to school and we can't play football. Can we have your little football instead, Number Ten, PLEEEAAASE?"

The littlest dragon looked thoughtful.

"We'll give you... one orange, two apples, three sandwiches, four boxes of juice, five packets of crisps, six grapes, seven red lollipops, eight chocolate biscuits, nine fairy cakes, and ten jelly dragon sweets," said his big brothers.

"Sorry," said the littlest dragon as he took his football and went off to play with his friends, "but I'm too little to eat all that food."

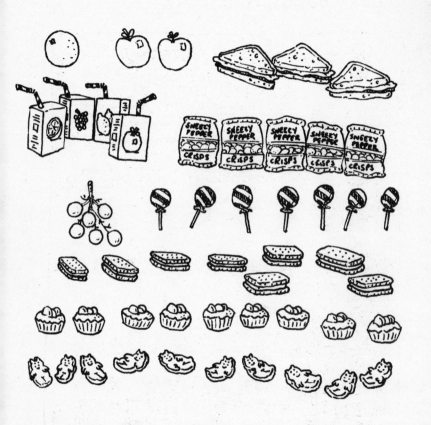

THE LITTLEST DRAGON
RUNS A RACE

The littlest dragon hurried home
from school one day waving a letter
in the air.

"There's to be a school fête," he
told his mum, "and Dragon McFeet
is presenting the prizes for the races.
I'm going to enter every one."

His mum smiled and read the
letter. "It costs fifty pence to enter
each race," she said. "How much
money have you got in your dragon
bank?"

"I don't know. I'll check," said the littlest dragon.

He emptied his dragon bank and counted five ten pence pieces.

"I've only got fifty pence," he said.

"That means I can only enter one race. I think I'll choose the flat race. I'll go and practise right now."

He went out into the garden and ran round it three times.

"You'll never win the flat race," scoffed big dragon brothers One, Two and Three. "Your legs are far too skinny. You'll be last. We'll be first."

"Oh dear," said the littlest dragon looking down at his legs. "Perhaps I'd better enter the sack race instead. I'll go and practise right now."

He went to the garden shed and got out an old sack. He climbed in and jumped round the garden four times.

"You'll never win the sack race," smirked big dragon brothers Seven, Eight and Nine. "Your legs are far too short. You'll be last. We'll be first."

"Oh dear," said the littlest dragon, looking down at his legs.

"Perhaps I'd better enter the egg and spoon race instead. I'll go and practise right now."

He went into the big cave kitchen
and asked his mum for a hard boiled
egg and a spoon. Then he ran round
and round the garden five times till
he was tired out. After all that, big
dragon brothers Four, Five and Six
appeared.

"You'll never win the egg and spoon race," said big dragon brother number Four. "Your legs are far too skinny and short. You'll be last. I'll be first."

"And don't even think about entering the three-legged race," said twin brothers Five and Six. "We're the same height and our legs are the same length. We're bound to win."

"Oh dear," said the littlest dragon. "Now which race am I going to enter?"

He checked the letter about the fête which his mum had stuck up on the kitchen wall. There was only one race left. It was the obstacle race. It came right after the pie-eating competition. That gave the littlest dragon his first idea.

"Mum," he said. "Could you bake lots and lots of our favourite apple pies for the pie-eating competition?"

"Certainly," smiled his mum. "I'll get some apples from the garden."

That gave the littlest dragon his second idea. He went out into the garden to see his dad.

"Dad, could you put out some obstacles in the garden for me to practise on for the obstacle race?"

"Certainly," said his dad, and put out a barrel which had been cut in half, an old climbing frame, and a potato sack open at both ends.

"Thank you," said the littlest dragon, and he climbed up and over and through everything six times.

The day of the fête arrived. The
littlest dragon hurried along to the
school playing fields with his fifty
pence for the obstacle race. His big
brothers laughed at him.

"You haven't a hope," they grinned.
"We're going to win all the races."

But they didn't.

Number One was second in the flat race. Number Eight was third in the sack race. The twins, Five and Six, fell over their feet in the three-legged race and were last.

"But we're bound to win the obstacle race," the big dragon brothers boasted.

"Remember, it's the pie-eating competition first," said the littlest dragon who then had his third and best idea. "Bet I can eat more of mum's apple pies than any of you," he said.

"Bet you can't," said his brothers and began to tuck in.

Big dragon brothers Seven, Eight and Nine ate four pies each. Big dragon brothers Four, Five and Six ate six pies each. Big dragon brothers Two and Three ate eight pies each, and biggest dragon brother, Number One, ate ten pies. All at once!

And they were so busy munching they didn't notice that the littlest dragon ate nothing at all.

At last it was time for the obstacle race to begin. The littlest dragon lined up beside his brothers and READY STEADY GO, he was off... through the barrels, over the climbing frames, through the sacks and over the finishing line... FIRST!

The littlest dragon looked back at
his brothers. They were all still
stuck in the barrels!

"You'll never win the obstacle
race," he grinned. "You're far too big
and fat."

Then he went up to receive his prize from his favourite football star, Dragon McFeet.

"Well done, littlest dragon," said Dragon McFeet, and presented him with a brand new football and a card which said...

DRAGON McFEET PROMISES
TO GIVE A FOOTBALL LESSON
TO THE WINNER OF THE
OBSTACLE RACE.

"That's me. That's me," cried the littlest dragon. Then he looked down at his legs. "You don't think my legs are far too skinny and short to play football, do you?"

"Of course not," smiled Dragon
McFeet. "I think they're just right."